ONE SOUL

ONE SOUL

VERONICA BROWN

J Merrill Publishing, Inc., Columbus 43207
www.JMerrillPublishingInc.com

Published 2021

Library of Congress Control Number: 2020921998
ISBN-13: 978-1-950719-60-0 (Paperback)
ISBN-13: 978-1-950719-59-4 (eBook)

Title: One Soul
Author: Veronica Brown

*To: **My ABBA GOD***

May you fill this book with your HOLY SPIRIT that your people will gain the joy of knowing that they too can win one soul.

To My Parents: George and Kathy Brown.

I love you both so very much! Thank you for encouraging me and praying for me when I couldn't pray for myself. Parents, you have selfless love, and the light of CHRIST is evidence through your life! Keep laughing, keep smiling, keep singing unto the LORD a new song!!

To My Siblings: Calvin, Georgette, Vanessa, and Jeremiah Brown

I am truly grateful for the close relationship that we have with one another. It is priceless, and I wouldn't trade it for the world! I love you all to life!

To JESUS, my KING!!!

Thank YOU for the great sacrifice that YOU have given so I and all others can have new life in YOU! Thank YOU so much for saving my soul!!!

CONTENTS

1

TAKING A STEP

Charlotte Maine is a vibrant lady who enjoys the simple things in life. She likes taking walks in the park no matter what the weather is. While at the park, Charlotte enjoys hearing the refreshing sound of the waterfall flowing from the middle of the lake. She enjoys seeing families out together having a fun time, and she especially likes to smell the hot dogs cooking from the small grills in the park.

Most importantly, Charlotte loves to spend time in her Aunt Melva's garden. She likes being in the sun and digging her hands through the dirt and soil. It makes her happy just to see the beautiful flowers grow each year. Blooming and blossoming from tulips, red roses, and lovely morning glories.

Her Aunt Melva is a strong woman full of wisdom. However, that wisdom that she possessed didn't happen overnight, but it came through many experiences of dos and don'ts. That's why Charlotte couldn't be more thankful for her Aunt Melva.

Anyone would think that Charlotte had it all together. However, Charlotte had a tremendous fear that has been plaguing her for years. She became mentally frozen when she tried to meet new people. One could think what made this vibrant and caring lady so fearful.

One day, Charlotte prayed and asked GOD for help to take this fear away.

When Charlotte was younger, she was picked on a lot. Although she wanted to be accepted by her peers, she was unacceptable. She felt like the scum on the back of a shoe. She often wondered, "Will anyone honestly want to be my friend? Or will I always be an outcast?" Charlotte's heart was hurting for connection and true friendships.

Charlotte's Aunt invited her to a community outreach and asked if she wouldn't mind working at the popcorn machine. She was excited to do this because she loves the smell of fresh popcorn popping.

All the volunteers huddle together at the community outreach to see where they would be stationed. The building was immaculate with windows all around it hosting the beautiful natural sunlight

A 75-year-old lady by the name of Ms. Kingston owned this beautiful place. Sadly, she was a widow, but her heart finds joy in serving the community which she had done for decades

"Charlotte, I want you to be the greeter at the doors."

"The greeter?" She asked as her face got flushed, and her hands began to sweat. Say something, she said to herself. Charlotte leaned over and whispered to Ms. Kingston. She was a little nervous about being upfront, and she would rather be in the background making popcorn as she was volunteered to do. Besides, she wasn't good around people. As a matter of fact, people terrified her, which is the main reason she works where she talks to customers over the phone instead of face-to-face.

Ms. Kingston puts her arms around Charlotte. "Alright, honey," she said, "give her a greeter's badge. The only way you're going to get over your fear of people is to be around them, and I promise you they won't bite." She chuckled.

Charlotte made her way through the volunteer line, but her heart felt like she was being thrown to the sharks.

A friendly lady named Julie was sitting at the table. "May I have your name, please?" Julie asked. Julie signed Charlotte in.

Charlotte made her way to the front of the big glass doors. A man named Victor was there cleaning the glass and setting up for the guest.

"Is this where the greeters meet," asked Charlotte.

Victor turned around and saw Charlotte. "Yes, and you are?"

"My name is Charlotte," she said, with her head down.

"Well, Charlotte. My name is Victor, and a beautiful lady like you should never put her head down."

Charlotte slowly lifts her head.

"So, where are you from," said Victor.

"I'm from the other part of town near Fina."

"Oh yes, I'm very familiar with that part of town. My grandma lives over there. She owns The Blue Wagon restaurant."

Charlotte joyously explains to Victor how much she likes that restaurant and how she really enjoys the pork chops and mango salad. They both are amazed at how small the world really is.

"Well, welcome aboard," he says as he shakes her hand.

A man's voice on the intercom came blaring through.

"Attention," he called. "I would like to personally thank you all for volunteering for our 7th annual community outreach. We will be opening the doors in 10 minutes."

The volunteers all scurried with excitement, putting the finishing touches on their stations.

"Are you ready," Victor asked.

"I'm so nervous," said Charlotte.

"Don't be," said Victor. "Let's practice."

Charlotte sat at the table near the door and took a deep breath. Victor stepped up to the table and pretended to be a guest! "Hi, welcome to the um, um I can't do this," said Charlotte.

"Yes, you can," Victor replied. Victor writes down a mini script for her, but everything in Charlotte wanted to run out of those doors. But then she would have run right into the guests who were already lined up outside of the doors. So, there was nothing else for her to do, but muster up the courage, take a deep breath, and start over. This time Charlotte aced it with the help of the script, of course.

"All right," a voice on the intercom begins to count down 10, 9, 8, 7, 6, 5, 4, 3, 2...

"Are you ready?" Victor asked.

"Yes," said Charlotte. Those big glass doors swung open as a flock of people came in from all walks of life and all ages. It was a sight to behold.

Victor worked hard at keeping things in order, and Charlotte worked diligently to make every guest feel welcomed. The sound of unity filled the air, and Charlotte was overflowing with joy in her heart. The community outreach was a huge success.

That night Charlotte pondered the day, and she was so grateful for how it all turned out. "GOD, thank you so much for this day, and thank you for giving me the strength to face my fear," said Charlotte.

2
—————

DESTINY AWAITS

Two months have passed, and it was a cool afternoon in the town of Fina. Charlotte was swinging on the porch at Aunt Melva's house.

Charlotte says, "Aunt Melva, I want you to take the truck and go pick up some food for us at the Blue Wagon." Aunt Melva handed Charlotte twenty dollars and the keys to the truck.

She enjoys driving that truck because it made her feel like she was somebody. She put on her favorite radio station and was jamming out to her favorite songs. "Thank you for tuning in to 91.9 FM, where you can find love, encouragement, and hope streaming from every note said an announcer on the radio. We are super excited to share with you that every Wednesday, 'Active Hearts' will be meeting from 6:00 pm-8:30 pm in their new location, Still Bend Mountain. As their motto has always been: Instead of being in church, we are going to go out and be the church! Let's go and reach somebody!"

"Hmmm... Active Hearts?" thought Charlotte.

Pop, pop, went the tire on the old esteem truck. "No," said Charlotte, as the truck came to a dreary stop.

She put on the blinkers and opened the door slowly. As she got out, cars were whizzing right past her.

Charlotte carefully made her way to the back of the truck and took out two bright neon green cones so the other cars would see her. "I'm sure glad I know how to change a tire," she said.

She pulled her hair up in a bun and got straight to work. After about 25 minutes of working hard, Charlotte was done. She felt a sense of accomplishment. "You still got it, Char," she said.

Just then, Charlotte's cell phone rang, but when she went to reach for it in her pocket, she realized she left it in the truck. Charlotte went to open the door of the truck, but it wouldn't budge. She pulled and pulled, but the door handle would not open. She looked in the truck. And sitting on the driver's seat were her keys! Her keychain was facing up at her with the colorful words, "Fear Not," looking up at her.

"This can't be happening," she said, shaking the door handle with all her might.

"Aunt Melva must be worried sick about me. Open, open, open," she shouted at the truck in frustration.

Just then, a rusty truck squeaks right up behind her. "Great, just what I need," she said sarcastically.

"Hi, are you alright?"

"Yes," Charlotte said with a bit of an attitude. "I'm fine."

"Charlotte?" asked Victor.

"Victor," she said with a sigh of relief.

"What's going on?" he asked. Charlotte explained to him what happened, and Victor was more than happy to help her. Charlotte called her Aunt and thanked Victor for his help.

"Are you going to be alright going home," asked Victor.

"Yeah, I'll be fine. Thank you. I really appreciate you stopping," she said while starting up the truck.

"No problem," said Victor, "and with it being you, that was a bonus for me." Charlotte looked away with a side smile.

"There goes that beautiful smile," said Victor. He looked at her as if he wanted to say something.

"Well, thanks again," said Charlotte.

"Umm, before you go," said Victor. "I know this is spur of the moment, but if you're not doing anything tomorrow night. I wanted to invite you to a meeting with the Active Hearts community. We will be meeting at our new location, Still Bend Mountain. I mean, since you did so well the last time; I thought that maybe you wanted to..."

"Yes," said Charlotte, I heard the announcement for it on the radio today, and it really stuck out to me."

"Well," said Victor, "let's just say I think you just bumped into destiny."

3

IT'S NOT ENOUGH

The meeting started, A lady with a southern accent came to the front.

"I would like to welcome you all to Active Hearts. My name is Gingerelli. I am the executive director of this gathering. Still, I couldn't have done any of this without the kindest heart that anyone could ever meet, my cousin, Victor!"

Everyone clapped as they looked his way. "Victor also brought a guest with him today. May we all welcome Charlotte." Everyone clapped. Charlotte's eyes got big as she saw all eyes on her.

"Charlotte, may you please stand up and let us know a little bit about you," said Gingerelli.

"What's your favorite movie," shouted Victor.

Charlotte's heart was beating fast as she stood up with all eyes on her. "My name is Charlotte. I live in the small town of Fina. My favorite movie, I will have to say, is Amazing Grace." The audience seemed to agree with her movie choice. Charlotte starts to walk back to her seat. However, to Charlotte's surprise, that little interview wasn't done yet.

"Why is that your favorite movie?" Gingerelli said.

"Umm, because it's a movie that is very encouraging and focuses on the power of purpose." She turned, again, to take her seat.

"Wow, that's really a good perspective," said Gingerelli. "May you elaborate? As a matter of fact, let's have you come to the front. I'm interested in hearing more. Don't y'all want to hear more, too?" said Gingerelli.

The clapping of the audience went right through Charlotte. Gingerelli handed her the microphone, and Charlotte paced to the front.

"Don't be nervous, Charlotte. We're all family here," said Victor.

Charlotte breathed deeply then spoke. "The power of purpose..." said Charlotte.

Just then, a buzz of the microphone sounded.

Charlotte tapped the microphone, trying to get the buzz to stop. Victor ran up to the front and handed Charlotte another microphone. "Thank you," she said.

Charlotte stood back from the microphone, cleared her throat, and started again.

"In the movie Amazing Grace, the power of purpose is what I would say is the forefront of the objective of the movie. Many of us have dealt with, and are dealing with, thinking we have missed the real reason we were created and put here on this earth.

This movie portrays that we all were inundated with purpose, and we can't get away from it. No matter what the element of our environment dictates. We will always be fueled by our purpose. It will be a huge fight, but if we take the time to hear purpose, which stirs on the inside of each of us, we will accomplish it! Thank you," she said.

Applause filled the air as Charlotte made her way back to her seat.

She was embraced by the arms of Victor, who smelled so good. Charlotte couldn't help but to just melt in his arms. It was like a big golden circle drawn around them and brought them together for such a time as this! They both took their seats.

"Wow, Charlotte," Victor whispered. "That was awesome. That is why we need you here."

Charlotte felt so connected at that very moment.

She became an asset to the Active Hearts community and served faithfully for five months. They had become like a second home to Charlotte. She gained many new connections - not only with those in the group but, with those living on the streets.

Charlotte and Victor became like two peas in a pod, from giving food to the people to handing out daily necessities every week. Anyone could see they were inseparable.

Charlotte especially enjoyed it when they talked on the phone. She really liked Victor and believed that he liked her, too. Still, both seemed a little nervous and didn't want to overstep their boundaries because Victor held a leadership role within the group. Although Charlotte truly believed that Victor would soon ask her out.

When Charlotte got home, she sat on her microfiber couch. The softness of the furniture seemed to seal her in coziness and comfort. "What a beautiful day," she said. To Charlotte, all was right with the world, and she was sure glad to be a part of it!

That night Charlotte could not sleep. She was tossing and turning all night.

Then she had a dream. The sun was shining brightly, and Charlotte was standing outside of the center, laughing, and talking with Victor and the people that they served each week.

Everyone seemed to be happy and full. Then suddenly, a man wearing an all blue coat came up to the tent where they were and shook Charlotte while saying, "It's not enough, it's not enough!"

Men with black masks came with poles of fire in their hands and started to run after the people burning them at the stake. Everyone was running for a place of safety, but no place seemed to be safe.

Just then Charlotte was pulled into a dark alley, but this pull was not a pull of any person; it was a strong, yet gentle pull.

She began to take flight through the alley then, immediately the dingy brick walls opened, and Charlotte began to soar. While soaring, Charlotte heard a voice above her saying, "CHRIST in you the hope of glory, glory, glory," and the voice started to fade.

Charlotte was awakened by a loud clap of thunder and a bright streak of light that seemed to light up her room. She stood up straight in her bed and fell to her knees.

"OH GOD," she cried. "Give me one soul. One soul a day that I can tell about you. One soul a day that I can lead to Jesus. Make me bold. Make me unafraid. OH GOD, give me one soul! In the name of Jesus, I ask and pray, amen."

Streams of tears covered Charlotte's face as she laid there in complete stillness.

The next morning Charlotte was leaving for work, and a very tall man came out of nowhere from behind her apartment complex. She was startled by him, but then realized that he is her upstairs neighbor's son.

"Hi, Jeffrey. Are you okay?" she asked because his eyes looked heavy.

"Yea, I'm just going through some hard times, but you are looking beautiful, Charlotte," he said.

Charlotte felt very uncomfortable. "Well, I must go, and I hope you have a better day." As Charlotte was making her way to her car, she felt that pull kind of like her dream, but fear pulled her right in her car.

Then she heard these words in her heart, "Tell him about Me!"

"Tell him about you, but LORD," Charlotte said. Suddenly, a boldness came over Charlotte, and she darted out of her car. "Jeffrey!" she shouted. Charlotte shared the gospel of JESUS with him. The conversation went so much better than she thought.

Jeffery asked GOD to forgive him of his sins and was willing to turn from them. He asked JESUS to be the Savior and LORD of his life. Charlotte gave him some materials to help him on his journey, and she included information about a men's group in which he could connect.

Charlotte was in awe to see that even Jeffrey's eyes, which were bloodshot red, changed to completely clear as they prayed. She could see that he had an encounter with GOD, and what was happening in the natural was just an indication of what was taking place in the SPIRIT of GOD.

After saying bye to Jeffrey, Charlotte got into her car. "Wow, GOD!" Charlotte said, "That was awesome! All he needed is you. GOD, only YOU." She pulled out of the parking space and headed to work.

When she got to her cubicle, she saw all her things were packed in a brown box.

"What's going on," Charlotte said to her co-worker.

They're downsizing and letting 50 people go.

"What do you mean by downsizing? This is a billion-dollar company. We are in Forbes."

"I'm sorry, Charlotte. Sorry no," she said and walked quickly to her supervisor's office.

"Mr. Baker, what…"

"I'm sorry this was a surprise to us all," he said.

"Is there anything I can do," asked Charlotte?

"I wish there were Charlotte. You are such a valuable worker in this company. It frustrates me to see you go. You are one of our top representatives, and you have helped so many of our customers. Your surveys are always 100%, and your attributes are through the roof. You have brought sunshine to this company with so many great ideas that have made us a very successful company. That is why I am so sorry to see you go."

"I don't understand," said Charlotte as she put her head down. "Please Mr. Baker, I can't lose my job."

Mr. Baker comes over to Charlotte and hugs her.

"It's not fair," said Charlotte.

"I know," said Mr. Baker, "but when corporations don't know the people that work for them on a personal level, they sometimes tend to make mistakes and, in this case, a huge one."

Charlotte slowly pulls away. "So there's nothing we can do?" she asked.

"I'm sorry," said Mr. Baker. "If you ever need a reference, just let me know."

Charlotte walks out the doors and goes back to her desk one last time as Nyle, the security guard, waits. Fifty people all step out in a single file line as if they were prisoners. The walk to those big revolving doors was the longest ever as each person turned in their badge and left the building.

"Charlotte..." said Nyle.

"I know," said Charlotte, "you're just doing your job. Believe me, I have watched a few people be escorted out of this place. I understand that it's protocol."

"You take care," said Nyle.

Charlotte said her goodbyes to the co-workers who became more like family to her. They all promised to keep in touch.

She looked back at the company that she was no longer a part of, the company that had become her second home, the place that will now be just a memory. A drizzle of rainfall began to drop as she walked to the parking garage. They got bigger and bigger and bigger until Charlotte was drenched from head to toe.

"You gotta be kidding me," she said. She ran to her car with her box in her hands. As she was running, she slipped and fell smack dab in the puddle of water. All she could hear was the piercing sound of the crack of her ankle. "Ouch!" said Charlotte. She tried to get up, but instead, she kept falling. At that very moment, Charlotte knew there was no use, so she just laid in the puddle.

"Oh my dear, are you alright?" asked a little old lady who was approaching her.

"Um," Charlotte said in pain.

"Stay right there. I'm going to get some help."

Charlotte tried to slide herself up, but her body just wouldn't cooperate. Tears began to flow from her eyes. "GOD why?" Charlotte said.

"Here I got someone to help," said the little old lady. A man came running towards Charlotte.

"Charlotte?" said Victor. "Wow, what happened to you?"

"It's a long story," she said in pain.

"Do you two know each other?" said the little old lady?

"Yes, quite well," said Victor.

"This is wonderful," said the nice old lady. "The LORD sure does work in mysterious ways."

"I guess, ouch," said Charlotte.

"Here, take my hand. I'm going to pull you up."

"You can't. I think I broke my ankle."

"Then I will carry you. Put your arms around my shoulder."

Charlotte wrapped her arms around Victor. The little old lady grabbed Charlotte's things, and all three of them walked to Victor's truck.

"Well, will you two be alright," asked the old lady.

"Yes, thank you so much," said Charlotte.

"You're so welcome. May the LORD be with you, dear."

Charlotte and Victor arrived quickly at the hospital. The waiting room was packed. They waited for two hours before she was called back, which wasn't bad for an emergency room. She was just glad that she had good health insurance, even though now she had no job.

"Charlotte Maine," the nurse called. "Is there a Charlotte Maine," she yelled?

"Over here," said Victor.

The nurse put Charlotte in a wheelchair.

"Are you coming back with her?" she asked.

"If she's alright with that," said Victor.

"Yes, that will be fine," said Charlotte.

As they made their way back, there were so many sick people waiting. Charlotte's heart went out to them, especially to the young lady who was sitting in the corner of the room with sunglasses on. She had a beautiful baby girl in a stroller right beside her.

"We have an emergency," said the nurse. "I'm sorry I will be back as soon as I can."

"This can't be happening right now," said Charlotte.

The nurse parked Charlotte right next to the young mother.

"Hi," said Charlotte.

"Hi, may I help you," the young mother said rudely.

Charlotte looked away.

The young mother got up and pushed the stroller to the nurse's station. "How long is this going to be," said the young mother.

"I'm sorry for your wait, ma'am." the nurse said. "We will get to you as soon as possible."

"Soon as possible? I've been sitting here for three hours. Just say it, it's because of my insurance you are putting me in the back of the line."

"Oh, no ma'am. We are just extremely busy."

"Extremely busy?" she said. "Y'all don't care nothing about nobody."

She went and sat back down with tears in her eyes.

"I'm sorry," said Charlotte.

"They don't care nothing about me," said the young mother. "It's all about the money, and I don't have that."

"Well, for whatever it's worth, I hope you get seen soon," said Charlotte.

"Yeah, if they change their system."

"Um, by the way, my name is Charlotte."

"Oh, I'm Starla."

"What a pretty name, and your little girl is so cute."

"Oh, thanks, but she's a handful."

"Aww, well, I'm sure you are a good mother."

"Her father doesn't think so."

She slowly removed her sunglasses. Charlotte saw the dreaded bruise on her eyes.

"He hates me, and he treats me like the scum on the back of his shoes. I do so much for him, and he hates me. "

"That is horrible," said Charlotte. "I'm so sorry. Have you gone to the authorities about this? Do you have anyone you can talk to?"

"No, I'm scared, and well, my family didn't like him from the start. Besides, I don't feel like hearing them say, I told you so! I mean, they don't know how it feels to be overlooked by men so much. Then I met him, and he told me the words that I longed to hear. He gave me the right looks and the right touch. Now I feel trapped in his web, and now, I'm pregnant, she said with her head down. It's all my fault! I don't know what to do. I'm so scared."

Charlotte tried to encourage her and let her know that she doesn't deserve to be treated like that. Starla's heart was broken. "I knew better," she said.

"Starla, we all have made choices that we shouldn't. But the way you are being used and abused, you don't have to stay in that kind of environment," said Charlotte. "and I'm sure your family just wants the best for you."

Starla explained to Charlotte how she didn't want to get him in trouble. "He is a good provider for my daughter and me," she said.

Charlotte handed Starla a business card. "What's this?" she asked.

"It's the number to a lady that helped me. Her name is Carol."

"Rescue House," said Starla reading the card. "Thanks, I could really use some rescuing. I'm such a mess right now."

"Starla, you are a daughter of GOD. You are royalty; that's your identity. The devil would want nothing more but to destroy you through this relationship."

"So, you're a Christian?" asked Starla.

"Umm...yes," said Charlotte.

Starla told Charlotte about her background in the church and how she was highly involved, but now she only felt a sense of worthlessness and shame.

Charlotte shared with Starla her story. "You see, I haven't always been walking the straight and narrow road. I, too, was in a relationship that almost took my life. It put so much fear in me."

She took a deep breath. "When I was younger, I was abused repeatedly. Because of this, I had a twisted view of love. For many years, I allowed people to do whatever they wanted with me. I also put myself in some situations that I am not proud of. Many nights I cried myself to sleep feeling dirty. I hated to even look at myself in the mirror. I was lost and so afraid. I even lost friends because of the way I was living.

One night I got on my knees, and I cried out to GOD. Even though I wasn't sure if HE would even hear someone like me. But I was desperate, and I needed help. All I could see is all the times that my great Aunt was up praying.

Night after night, I prayed. Then one day a co-worker of mine invited me to a coffee house, and it was so much fun and delicious she laughed but, one thing that I will never forget is the play that was performed that night. I saw the power of GOD displayed in such a way that I had never known before.

From there, I sensed the powerful arms of JESUS wrapped me up like a warm blanket. GOD became so real to me! I found out that HE loves me, and I could be His daughter, she said with tears.

I wanted that so much because I lost my Dad at the age of 14 am my great Aunt and uncle took me in."

Starla expressed her condolences to Charlotte.

"Wow," said Starla. "I would have never thought that just by looking at you. You seem like you have it all together well, except for your ankle right now."

They both laughed. "Girl," said Charlotte, "looks can be deceiving."

Starla agreed. "If you don't mind me asking, what happened to your mom?"

"I never had a real relationship with my mom because she was so strung out on drugs, she didn't want to have anything to do with me. However, that night after the play, I gave my life to JESUS. I mean, I had so many questions about GOD, but that night it was like all my questions were answered in a moment! Then through my co-worker, I met my mentor Carol, and I became a part of Rescue House." Starla looked at the business card.

"I didn't realize it until now that GOD had orchestrated that meeting. What GOD had deposited in Carol is what I needed for true deliverance to take place in my life. I was given a safe place to live, and my life began to turn around. Wow, said Starla, it's nice to know that I'm not alone. We all have a story," said Charlotte.

"And no, you're not alone. GOD has not forgotten you, but I left HIM," said Starla.

"Starla, GOD loves you, and yes, it's our sin that separates us from HIM. We all have sinned and come short of GOD'S glory. Like, in a volleyball game, when you hit the ball, hoping it will go over the net, but instead it hits the net, and the referee calls out short! We all deserve to be isolated from GOD, and we all deserve hell because of the wrong we have done. However, GOD doesn't want anyone to perish and be eternally separated and tormented forever. Hell was not made for people. It was prepared for the devil and his demons, not for us. However, hell is the home for unconfessed and unrepented sin."

"Hell is for those who reject JESUS."

"I don't want to go to hell," said Starla.

"Neither does GOD," said Charlotte.

"That is precisely why JESUS came. JESUS came down to the earth in human flesh, he was GOD in the flesh."

"The blood that JESUS shed when he died on the cross cleanses you from all your sins. It is your key. It is your access to GOD the FATHER. Just like when someone pays your admission fee at the amusement park or pays for your dinner. The way has already been paid through JESUS. All you have to do is come. Repent and be willing to turn from your sin and let JESUS be the LORD and Savior of your life. You can be reconciled back to GOD and brought into a personal relationship with HIM through JESUS. Also, the resurrection of JESUS provides you with a newness of life! It's that simple. Repent, believe the gospel, and you shall be saved."

"I want GOD so much," said Starla. "I really do need HIM."

"May I pray with you," asked Charlotte.

"Yes, please do," said Starla.

Starla and Charlotte prayed, and Starla gave her life to the LORD.

Charlotte gave Starla a big hug and said, "Starla, today start a new chapter of your life of GOD'S redeeming power."

Just then, Charlotte's name was called to see the doctor. "Wow, I almost forgot I was here," she said.

Starla thanked Charlotte as she was being wheeled back to the room.

While she was in the room, she heard Starla's name being called on the intercom. "Oh, thank YOU, LORD," she said to herself.

The doctor checked her out and got some x-rays taken, and finally, it was time for Charlotte to get discharged. Good news said the doctor. Your ankle is not broken, only sprained.

"Thank GOD," said Victor.

"Thank GOD indeed!" exclaimed Charlotte. She was finally released, and Victor stayed right by her side. They made their way to the door.

"That was nice. What you did for Starla back there? You have so much compassion. You are one of a kind," said Victor.

"It was GOD'S HOLY SPIRIT," said Charlotte. "I'm just as amazed. I just really wish I could have done more," she said.

"Charlotte, GOD spoke through you. I could see HIS love wrapping all around her. You brought the light of CHRIST right into her darkness. CHRIST in you, the hope of glory," said Victor.

Charlotte immediately remembered her dream.

"Who's to say that all this happened just for one soul," said Victor.

"Charlotte was bursting with joy on the inside, thank you GOD," she said.

4

──────

HAPPY BIRTHDAY

It had been a long road for Charlotte, but she was fully recovered. She couldn't have been any more grateful for how much help she had received from her family and friends. From giving her rides to cooking her dinners, Charlotte was well taken care of. Charlotte and Victor spent so much time together. It seemed as if the golden circle around them was getting even bigger. Victor was so kindhearted, and he treated Charlotte like a pearl that she is.

"Charlotte, you sure do have some nice friends," said Aunt Melva. "GOD has turned so many things around for you. You're so involved with the community now. Charlotte, you are a whole new person like a caterpillar into a butterfly."

Charlotte smiled at Aunt Melva. "I can't begin to tell you how I feel. It's like I wake up just wanting to bring sons and daughters back to GOD. My prayer is that each day GOD will give me one soul and that I will be a laborer in HIS harvest. Even though there have been some inconveniences, it all has been worth it."

Aunt Melva kindly reminded Charlotte that her steps are ordered by the LORD.

Just then, Charlotte's phone rang. "Hello, this is her. Thank you so much. Yes sir. I will check my email. See you on Monday bye."

Charlotte could hardly contain her excitement. "Aunt Melva," she shouted. "I got the job! I will be working at Winners Co. I start immediately!"

"Well, Monday morning!" Aunt Melva congratulated Charlotte.

Charlotte was so happy to be offered the first shift. It will be a significant change from the second shift she used to work, and she was especially excited to be off on the weekends.

"Well, just make sure you give yourself plenty of time to adjust to waking up early," said aunt Melva.

Charlotte happily explained to her Aunt that rising early is nothing that prayer and coffee can't handle.

"I'm so proud of you, sweetie," said aunt Melva.

"Thank you. I got to go and call Victor!"

"Victor?" asked Aunt Melva.

"Yea, I really like him," said Charlotte. "I think he may be the one!"

"Well, the LORD will reveal HIS perfect will in due time," said Aunt Melva.

"I know He will," Charlotte said, excitedly. "I mean, we are such a good match, and we have done so much together. I never felt a connection like this before, with anyone else."

Aunt Melva smiled and said, "HE will reveal."

Charlotte was so excited to call Victor, but she didn't even have to pull up his number because he was calling her.

"Hi, Victor, I was just about to call you. We are so in sync!" said Charlotte.

"Well, you first," said Victor.

"I got the job!"

"You got the job that is so awesome, Charlotte! It couldn't have come at a much better time now that you are fully recovered. No one deserves it more," said Victor.

"Thank you," said Charlotte. "I really do appreciate you, Victor. I mean from the hospital to cooking me meals to washing the dishes, I thank you so much."

Victor humbly told her that it was no problem and that it was his pleasure. "Besides," he said, "that's what friends are for."

"Friends," Charlotte said to herself that word had plagued Charlotte's heart more than once. A hushed tone was heard on the phone.

"Charlotte, I have something to tell you."

"Is everything alright," asked Charlotte?

"Yes, everything is great. I have been accepted to go into the army!"

"The army?" said Charlotte with a shocking voice.

"Yes, it's something I have wanted to do for a very long time. I thought you would be happy for me."

"I just... We're going to miss you," said Charlotte.

"I'm going to miss everyone, too," he said.

"When do you leave," Charlotte asked.

"Next month on March 24th, I start boot camp."

"Wow, that's my birthday," said Charlotte.

"Well, you and I will have to celebrate before I go," said Victor.

Charlotte's mind wanted to say what's the point, but her words spoke, "I would like that."

"It looks like we both are getting what we want," said Victor.

"Yeah," said Charlotte.

Deep inside, she just wanted to shout it on the rooftops and tell him how much she wanted to be with him, but her thoughts were quickly cut off when Victor said, "GOD sure does reveal HIS will." Charlotte remembered the words her Aunt had just said to her.

They said their goodbyes as Charlotte's heart sunk within her. She felt as if the golden circle around them had burst right before her eyes.

Charlotte sat down at the kitchen table and just stared into space.

"What's the matter," Aunt Melva asked?

"Oh, Aunt Melva," she said, "GOD has revealed HIS will,"

5

NOT TOO FAR FROM HOME

It's been months since Victor had left for the army, and Charlotte started her new job. The weekly outreaches were going well within the Active Hearts community, and Gingerelli was very welcoming to Charlotte's ideas. Charlotte was faithful to pray every day that GOD would let her connect to one soul and that she may tell them about the great news of the salvation of JESUS!

The next day at the center, Gingerelli said, "Charlotte, I would like you to meet someone."

Charlotte turned around and could not believe who she saw. "Mom!" she said.

"Wow, this is your mom," said Gingerelli. "What a small world."

"I'm sorry to interrupt," said one of the volunteers, "but Gingerelli, we have a little situation in the back."

"Oh well, duty calls," said Gingerelli, "but this is so great!"

"Charlotte, I can't believe it's you," said her mom, reaching out to hug her, but Charlotte just pulled away.

"What are you doing here?" she asked.

"I'm here with my daughter."

"I'm sorry, what? Your daughter?" said Charlotte.

"Yes, she's right over there. Right when Charlotte's Mom was pointing, a loud sound of canned goods was heard falling from the shelf."

"I'm sorry," said Charlotte, "excuse me." Charlotte hurried to the shelf where some of the people were standing.

"I'm so sorry," said the lady as she was frantically picking up the cans. Charlotte could not believe who it was.

Starla said, "Charlotte." Starla was so excited to see her, but she was even more embarrassed for all the cans that were on the floor. "I'm so sorry about all this mess. My little one here loves touching everything."

Charlotte assured Starla that she had nothing to worry about. She was just glad that they were alright. Starla thanked Charlotte for connecting her with Carol through Rescue House. She told her how she is no longer in that relationship and how she now works in a management position. "GOD has been so good to us," she said. Charlotte was amazed, Starla was like a brand-new person. I'm now living with my-

Just then, Charlotte's Mom came over. "Great, I see you two have met."

"Wait a minute. Do you know her?" asked Charlotte.

"She's my daughter," Charlotte's Mom said.

"Your daughter?" said Charlotte.

"Hold up, then that means we're sisters," said Starla. Starla was thrilled. "Mom, I didn't even know you were married before, does Dad know."

"Yes, he knows, but that was my other life."

"Your other life?" said Charlotte.

"I didn't mean it like that," said her mom.

"I'm sorry I need to go," said Charlotte as she walked away, trying to fight back the tears.

Charlotte's Mom called out to her. "Wait! I didn't mean it that way. I know I haven't been a good Mother to you. I have been downright horrible. I can't even imagine how you must have felt growing up without a Mother. I should have never done that to you or your Dad."

Tears began to fall from Charlotte's eyes as she quickly wiped them away.

"When those drugs she whispered started to take over my life, I didn't have any control. I couldn't even see straight half of the time. Those were the most horrific years of my life that almost took me out. But I'm so glad that it didn't, or I would not have had this moment with you, and for whatever it's worth, Charlotte, I'm so sorry."

Charlotte's mind begins to cloud up. She felt a sense of worthlessness come over her.

"Don't you worry about me," she said. "I'm just your other life."

Charlotte walked away, thinking about all the things her mom missed in her life, and even though she wanted to embrace her mom, she just couldn't find the strength. She walks to the back office and shuts the door behind her. Her heart was breaking in pieces. The wound she thought was healed was now freshly opened, and the tears she tried to suppress came streaming down her face.

Just then, Gingerelli came in handing Charlotte a note.

"What's this?" said Charlotte.

"It's from your mom," said Gingerelli. "Charlotte, what's wrong?" She asks reluctantly, not wanting to pry.

"My mom abandoned me when I was younger. She missed my homecoming, she missed my prom, my high school, and college graduation. She wasn't there to even show me how to put on my makeup. And, my first breakup, I had to suffer through that alone," she said crying.

"I'm sorry," said Gingerelli. "Is there anything I can do for you?"

"No, I just need to be alone," said Charlotte.

Gingerelli handed Charlotte a tissue box and put the letter on the table.

"Okay, take all the time you need. And, umm, also I know you may not want to hear this right now, but this may be your one soul."

She was right Charlotte did not want to hear that at all.

Charlotte went straight on her knees. "GOD why is this happening to me? Haven't I suffered enough? GOD, please help me!"

After praying a 911 prayer, she got up and bumped right into the table. "Ouch!!" she exclaimed. Her eyes landed right on the letter Gingerelli left on the table.

Charlotte slowly opens and reads the letter. She also noticed her mom's phone number on the note. "There is no way I'm calling her. It's too late, Mom," she said.

6

EYES OPEN

A few months had passed, and everything was going well for Charlotte at her new job. She's already received a pay raise. However, in her heart, she was still harboring unforgiveness towards her mom. She just refused to forgive her; besides, she had every right to feel this way.

She just wanted to move on with her life, and that is what she did, so she thought.

That night Charlotte had a dream about her mom and how the unseen evil world of drug addiction was tormenting her mom. And no matter what her mom tried to do she just couldn't get free. She watched as the evil force gripped her mom even more. She saw her mom fighting for her life as she was being taken away and dragged like a rag doll.

Charlotte shouted for her mom and ran to save her, but every time she got close, something would throw Charlotte down. She was determined to save her mom. So, she reached out her hand, and her mom reached back. Then something huge and startling kicked Charlotte back where she started, and her mom could no longer be seen. All she could hear was her screams in the distance.

Charlotte woke up, and her heart was beating fast. "No, no," she said. "GOD, I'm so sorry."

That day at work, Charlotte could not get her mom out of her mind the moment her break came she reached into her purse and pull her Mother's number out which was balled up at the bottom of her purse. She quickly opened the letter and called her mom.

Charlotte and her Mom met at the coffee shop. They both order a Grande mint hot chocolate. The coffee shop was bustling. The waitress said that she would bring their drinks to them. So, Charlotte and her Mom went to find a seat.

"Thank you so much for meeting me here," said Charlotte.

"I'm just glad you called me," said her mom. Charlotte didn't know what to say, but she knew it was now or never.

"Um, I just wanted to say how sorry I am for the way I acted and that I genuinely do forgive you."

"Charlotte, thank you so much. I can't even begin to tell you how much it pains my heart when I think about what I've done to you and your Dad. I wish I could make it up to you, Charlotte. I'm so sorry, she reaches out and takes her hand. I hope we can start anew."

"I would like that. I would like that so much," Charlotte cried.

Charlotte's mom took a napkin and gently wiped the tears from Charlotte's eyes. "I love you, my daughter."

The waitress was standing right there with their hot chocolate. "Aww, this is so sweet," she said. "I wish I had a close relationship with my mom, but I will never speak to her again. Anyways, here's y'all drinks."

"Um, I don't know your story, and I'm sure you have every right to be mad at your mom, but I would encourage you to reach out to her. You never know what she's up against."

"Well, with all due respect," said the waitress with an attitude. "It's going to have to take an act of GOD to make me forgive her."

"Oh, HE will," said Charlotte. "Thank you for our drinks."

"Yeah, you're welcome," said the waitress, as she walked away.

"Charlotte, thank you so much your forgiveness means the world to me. What made you change your mind."

"Well, let's just say it was an act of GOD," she laughed.

"I really want GOD in my life. I have seen such a change in Starla ever since she started following GOD. I mean, I don't understand it all, but I know I need HIM."

"Believe me, Mom, you don't have to be a scholar to come to GOD because if that were the case, none of us would be able to. It's a matter of putting your faith in JESUS. Admitting that you're a sinner in need of a Savior and being willing to turn from your sins and to turn to GOD. Scripture says that if you confess with your mouth the LORD JESUS and believe in your heart that GOD has raised HIM from the dead, you shall be saved. The blood of JESUS is enough to cleanse you and purify you and bring you back to GOD, who is your FATHER. The way has been made through JESUS. All you have to do is come."

"Will you pray with me, dear?" her mom asked.

"It will be my honor," said Charlotte.

Charlotte and her Mom prayed together.

"Wow, I feel like a brand-new person," said her mom. "Oh, thank you, JESUS, and thank you, Charlotte, for praying with me. I'm so happy."

Charlotte was overwhelmed with joy! "Now, we have each other," she said.

"And I have my daughter back," said her mom.

Charlotte's mom invited her over for lunch and was very curious about how she and Starla met. Charlotte promised that she would explain it all. At that moment, Charlotte's mom's phone rang, and it was Starla. She was in labor. Charlotte and her Mom quickly left the coffee shop.

Charlotte had a great time with her mom and her sister. That night before going to bed, Charlotte got down on her knees and thanked GOD for the restoration of her family.

❤It was almost three months since Charlotte reunited with her family. One Saturday morning, Charlotte got a call from Gingerelli. She told Charlotte that she had something very important to share with her.

They decided to meet at Charlotte's favorite spot, the park. When Charlotte arrived, the grills were scenting the park as usual. Many families were out splashing around in the waterfall!

Charlotte saw Gingerelli from afar, but her Mom, Starla, and Aunt Melva were there to her surprise.

"What are you all doing here," Charlotte asked.

Aunt Melva gave Charlotte a bouquet, and her Mom gave her a gift bag that glistened in the sun.

"Open the bag," Starla said excitedly.

Charlotte opens the bag, still unsure of what was going on. But as she opened the bag, there was a huge gold key.

"I don't understand," said Charlotte.

"Maybe this will help," said Gingerelli.

Just then, Victor came down the path with another gift for Charlotte.

"Victor," Charlotte said in astonishment.

Victor hugged Charlotte.

"Charlotte," he said, "we would like to present you with this plaque of our appreciation for your servanthood in our community, and we would like you to be the Executive Director of Active Hearts."

"Me," said Charlotte. "But what about Gingerelli? she asked.

"My husband was offered a job in Tennessee, so I will be moving in a few weeks," said Gingerelli. "Victor and I decided you will be the best person for the job."

Charlotte could not believe her ears, and she surely couldn't believe that Victor was standing right by her. She was honored to receive this new position. Everyone clapped and congratulated Charlotte.

"It looks like everything has come around full circle," said Victor.

"It sure has," said Charlotte.

Charlotte was so grateful for the opportunity. Many people were coming to the LORD and receiving help from the Active Hearts community in which she later called "One Soul."

> And every creature which is in heaven, and on the earth, and under the earth, and such as are in the sea, and all that are in them, heard I saying, Blessing, and honor, and glory, and power, be unto HIM (GOD) that sits upon the throne, and unto the LAMB (JESUS) forever and ever.

> -Revelation: 5:13

ABOUT THE AUTHOR

Veronica Brown is a native of Pennsylvania and now resides in Ohio. While in Pennsylvania, she served in the children's ministry, praise and worship team and was a part of the evangelistic team at York Christian Fellowship. Veronica also worked as a childcare/schoolteacher for over a decade. She received her CDA, Montessori Teaching Diploma, and certificates in Professional Development, through Penn State Better Kid Care Program.

Veronica sensed a strong call to come to Ohio and attend Valor Christian College. Although it took ten years for her to come to Ohio, by the grace of GOD that dream and calling was fulfilled.

Veronica graduated from Valor Christian College in 2018 and received an associate degree in Evangelism. She has worked as a preschool teacher at a local school in Ohio. Veronica's heart is for people to know the love of JESUS.

facebook.com/veronica.brown.9678

www.ingramcontent.com/pod-product-compliance
Lightning Source LLC
Chambersburg PA
CBHW060806210726
48292CB00013B/1870